TEEN TITANS
BEAST BOY *loves* RAVEN

t Alameda Ave., Burbank, CA 91505
unications, Crawfordsville, IN, USA. 5/6/22.

86-2

PEFC Certified
This product is from sustainably managed forests and controlled sources
www.pefc.org

Library of Congress Cataloging-in-Publication Data

Names: Garcia, Kami, writer. | Picolo, Gabriel, artist. | Haynes, Rob, artist. | Calderon, David, colourist. | Downie, Gabriela, letterer.
Title: Teen Titans : Beast Boy loves Raven / writer, Kami Garcia ; artist, Gabriel Picolo with Rob Haynes ; colorist, David Calderon ; letterer, Gabriela Downie.
Description: Burbank, CA : DC Comics, [2021] | Audience: Ages 13-17 | Audience: Grades 10-12 | Summary: While Raven Roth is finding a way to get rid of her demon father Trigon, Garfield Logan is understanding his newly found shapeshifting ability, and when their paths cross in Nashville they both feel a strong connection to one another.
Identifiers: LCCN 2021025265 | ISBN 9781779503862 (trade paperback)
Subjects: CYAC: Graphic novels. | Superheroes--Fiction. | Ability--Fiction. | Love--Fiction. | LCGFT: Superhero comics. | Romance comics. | Graphic novels
Classification: LCC PZ7.7.G366 Tc 2021 | DDC 741.5/973--dc23
LC record available at https://lccn.loc.gov/2021025265

WRITER
kami ga

ARTIST
gabriel pi

WITH
rob haynes

COLORIST
david caldero

LETTERER
gabriela downie

Raven created by
Marv Wolfman and George P

Beast Boy created by Arnold

TEEN TITANS: BEAST BO

Published by DC Comic
All characters, their di
this publication are tr
incidents featured in t
not read or accept un
DC – a WarnerMedia C

DC Comics, 2900 We
Printed by LSC Comm
Second Printing.
ISBN: 978-1-77950-3

Dear Reader,

Raven and Beast Boy are two of our all-time favorite characters. They remind us so much of ourselves as teens. They're both trying to figure out who they are and how they fit into a world that feels so different from themselves. They are just starting to embrace what makes them unique—to see their differences as strengths instead of weaknesses. But it's not easy, and they don't always get it right. Finding someone to connect with makes all those things easier, and that's what this book is about—friendship, found family, first love, and finding the courage to define ourselves in a world that constantly tells us who we should be. We have met so many of you in person or online, and we want Raven and Beast Boy to feel as brave and inspiring as all of you.

Thank you for reading.

Kami Garcia & Gabriel Picolo

CHAPTER 1: TWO OF A KIND
ON A TRAIN IN TENNESSEE
NOTE TO SELF,
FOUR MONTHS AGO, I LOST MY FOSTER MOM AND MY MEMORY ON THE SAME HORRIBLE NIGHT. I MOVED TO NEW ORLEANS TO LIVE WITH MOM'S SISTER, NATALIA, AND HER DAUGHTER, MAX. I DIDN'T THINK MY LIFE COULD GET ANY MORE COMPLICATED, BUT I WAS WRONG.
I'M WRITING THIS DOWN BECAUSE WITH MY LUCK, I MIGHT SLIP IN THE SHOWER AND BUMP MY HEAD AND LOSE MY MEMORY AGAIN. IF I DO, THERE'S ONE THING I CAN'T AFFORD TO FORGET. MY FATHER IS A DEMON. HE'S TRAPPED IN THE JEWEL I WEAR AROUND MY NECK AND HE WANTS TO TAKE CONTROL OF ME.
BLACK IS MY HAPPY COLOR

Raven
BLACK IS MY HAPPY COLOR
Do not resist, Raven.
Share your power with me until I regain my strength.
I'm not...sharing... anything with you.
You will.

GASP
BLACK IS MY HAPPY COLOR
I hope one day I'll be free of my monster.
DRACULA

When your foster sister says she's going to a strange city alone to meet a sketchy guy who claims he has the answer to her problems, you have two choices.
Let her go alone and hope for the best...
...or follow her and watch her back.
I'm not really a hope-for-the-best kind of girl.

Miss me already?
Bored to death yet?
No.
Maybe a little.
I could catch the next train and meet you in Nashville.
You'd have more fun with me around.
Not if Trigon uses my powers to break free again.
We can have fun after I figure out how to get rid of Trigon.

ON A BUS IN TENNESSEE
What if Slade can't help me? I've gotta figure out how this whole changing-into-animals thing works.
Slade
(555)321-2040
DINGG
MOM
Dad & I know you're upset.
Pls call. We love you.
HER BIV ORE
HYPE
My parents lied to me. Did they know what would happen if I stopped taking the fake supplements they were giving me?
I need some time to make sense of all this. You get it, don't you, buddy?

And she doesn't notice me.
I don't think it fits.
Nobody asked you.
WUNK

ALABAMA
PHEW!
Ask if she's okay.
Figures.

Welcome to Nashville.
Union Station
1:46 PM

I can do this.

I can do this.

MUSIC ROW
I know how to stop Trigon. Slade
You could've mentioned you were out of town *before* I came up here, Slade.
What am I supposed to do for two days?
Whatever teenagers do...drink overpriced coffee, go sightseeing, and post ridiculous selfies.
I don't even know what you look like. How will I find you?
I'll find you.
More information that conveys zero actual information. Perfect.
Wish I could bail. But Slade is the only person who might know how to get rid of Trigon.
Even though my father is gone, one thing won't change.
I'll still be half demon.

BBQ
DANCE
EAT
ALL NIGHT
NEW MUSIC
RIBS
BAR & GRILL
Everything here is so colorful.
BEST
IN TOWN
BARBEQUE
BBQ
LOVE
FADES
IS
BIG DADDY'S
BAR·B·QUE DRUGS
At least there are lots of places to eat. I'm starving.
Good thing I like barbecue.
BAR-B-QUE

I've got two days to kill before I meet Slade. Might as well try to have fun.
NASHVILLE
KING KONG
Things to Do on Music Row...
Go to a honky-tonk and eat barbecue. Those sound good.
THREE ROADS
MUSIC CITY
NEW RECORD S
BAR
Karaoke UPSTAIRS
ATM
SALO
OPEN 24 HRS
Bar
HONKY TONK
ATM
21+ ADULTS ONLY
That could be a problem.
OPEN 24 HRS
Bar
HONKY TONK
ATM
21+ ADULTS ONLY

Bet I'd look older in a cowboy hat.
HAT & BOOT
HONKY TONK
I.D.?
This is a funny story...

CHAPTER 2: GIRL IN BLACK

He's kinda cute minus the hat.
If I was looking for another guy, who would just end up lying to me.
13
10
13
10
Wait. This isn't what I...ordered.
I think that's mine and they gave me yours. I'm a vegetarian.
BLACK IS MY HAPPY
DRACULA

Since when are hot dogs vegetarian? If you're going to lie, at least put some effort into it.
It's a *vegan* dog.
In a Nashville barbecue place? Nice try.
BLACK IS MY HAPPY COLOR
Did you just pull my hair?
What is this, second grade?

It wasn't me.
See ya around... or not.
SEATING
BLACK IS HA COLOR
Thanks for blowing my chance, Kong.
EEEK
Is this a regular hot dog?
'Cuz I'm a vegetarian.
I don't eat meat.
That's not *meat*, darlin'. Ribs are meat. Brisket is meat.
That is a *hot dog*.
Right.
There goes my dream girl.
TONIGHT
NASHVILLE
Bar
WHISKEY
BBQ
OPEN

GUITAR
MOTEL
FREE INTERNET
LOW RATES
Cash rate is sixty a night.
Then one night, please.
It looks like Elvis Presley's bedroom exploded in here.

SWIP
WIPES
192
Drastic situations call for drastic measures.
YOU'RE USING MY

Ole Opry
MOTEL
Not bad for forty bucks.
You're picky for a monkey who was living in a cage a month ago.
KING KONG
SPLATT

THE NEXT DAY
This is it—the Country Music Hall of Fame.
PLANT POWERED
TH ENTRANCE

How did I end up here?
How cool is this?
PLANT POWERED

ZZZZ
MUSEUM GUIDE

ONE WAY
WALK
We could've had so much fun if Raven had let me come with her.
Best friends. Cousins. Foster sisters.
The two of us against the world...or just against Trigon.

CLAP
CLAP

THUMP!
Hello. I'm standing here. Try saying "excuse me" next time.
WE SELL BOOKS
24hr LAUNDROMA
SELF SERVICE

Come on. Move.
No! I can't lose her.

CHAPTER 3: KNIGHT IN TARNISHED ARMOR
latte love
There she is, Kong!
Don't screw things up for me this time.
NEW!
latte love
HYPE
That'll be four-eighty.
Total due....
Sorry...I can't find my wallet.

I've got it.
It has to be here.
Tourists have reported pickpockets around here for the last few weeks.
DRACULA
Here you go.
PLANT POWERED
You didn't have to...but thanks.
Someone stole my wallet.
Oh My Goth
You okay?

I'm fine.
You don't look fine.
Is that a monkey?
GARPHIL
Yep. His name is Kong. He's the one who pulled your hair in the restaurant.
I'm Gar, by the way.
Raven.
He's pretty cute.
He knows it.

It's getting late.
Do you have a way home?
Is there somebody you can call?
owell
GARPHY
<<Tax Invoice>>
I'm from New Orleans.
I could call my foster sister, but she was already worried about me coming here alone.
Why am I telling him this?
Where are you staying? I'll walk you.
I'm meeting someone, but he won't be here for two days. I was going to stay in a hotel, but...
Probably her boyfriend. A girl this cool can't be single.

I've got a room. You can crash there.
Nice try.
latte love
It's early. Let's hit another bar.
I wouldn't mind getting her alone.
Why am I hearing his thoughts?
This hasn't happened since I banished Trigon.

Back off.
PLANT POWERED
Whatever you say.
Do I look like a damsel in distress?
Huh?

I don't need a guy to swoop in and rescue me.
I'm capable of standing up for myself.
Sorry.
Where are you gonna stay?
Not your problem.
Watch out!
Ahhh!
Are you all right?
My offer stands.

I swear I'm not hitting on you.
You're probably dating someone anyway. I'm just trying to be nice.
How dangerous can a guy with green hair and a pet monkey be?
I bet that's what every girl thinks right before a harmless-looking guy kidnaps her.
But I'm not like other girls.
I can't afford to underestimate anyone again.

MOTEL
Everything is fine, Max. I just need you to transfer money into my account.
I'm in Nashville. Where else would I be?
You're acting weird. I'll call you tomorrow.
Max
Ta-da.
Wow. It looks like...
PLANT POWERED
An old lady's attic?
Pretty much.

So...um...wanna watch T.V.?
Sure. Whatever.
I love you.
I'm not in the mood for T.V.

I'll sleep on the floor.
Because you're a guy?
It's your room. You take the bed.

In a supernatural apocalypse, would you rather face zombies or vampires?
Excuse me?
C'mon.

Vampires.
Wrong.
Vampires are smarter and faster. You'd have a better chance against a zombie.
DRACUL
True. But if I lose, I'd rather turn into a vampire than a brain-eating zombie.
Perfect answer.
G'night, Raven.
Good night.
PLANT POWERED

5:30 A.M.
You cannot imprison me forever. When you make a mistake I will be waiting.
Stay away from me. Stay away!
What happened?

Raven? Wake up. You're having a nightmare.
Stay away from me!
Oh My Goth

Bad dream. Sorry I woke you up.
Could this be more embarrassing?
Wanna talk about it?
Stupid question. Too personal.
PLANT POWER
I don't remember it.

I should take off.
Now that I made a fool of myself.
You don't have to leave.
Thanks for letting me crash.
Where are you gonna go this early?
Oh My Goth

CHAPTER 4: LIES AND LINE DANCING
Why am I having nightmares about Trigon again? Is he getting stronger?
ATM
Maybe it's because I'm waiting for Slade, the mystery man, to show up and tell me what he knows.
Welcome!
DR JEKYLL AND HYDE
Even if I get rid of Trigon, what about my dark side?

Thank you.
latte love

Is running into you here a coincidence?
e love
I'm not a stalker if that's what you're asking.
Why'd you take off?
I'm not good at accepting help, I guess.
Not a total cop-out.
Oh My Goth

TWO HOURS LATER
If you could only eat one food for the rest of your life, what would it be?
Chinese food. How about you?
That's more than one food, but okay.
I'd pick pizza.

BZZZ
SLADE
Tied up helping another kid. Be there soon.
Soon? Is he talking days?
RAVEN
when??
hello??
Be right back.
Oh My Goth

BZZZ
10:21
SLADE
Helping another kid. Need a few more days.
BEAST BOY
it's all good
Everything okay?
The guy I'm meeting won't be here for a few days.
Lucky for you I've got this.
The NASHVILLE GUIDE

Bar
The book says this place has epic drinks.
Sightseeing is so cheesy.
It reminds me of Tommy, and my lying ex is the last person I want to think about.
Only if you're with the wrong person. I'm an awesome tour guide.
I read we should have the brunch for two.
Minus the alcohol. You got it.
MENU
Letting you order first just 'cuz you're a girl would be sexist.
No problem.
Oh My
MENU

Brunch for two.
Are those chickens? I'm a vegetarian.
Do you have any vegetarian options?
Coming right up.
THREE VERY LONG MINUTES LATER...
One vegetarian plate.
Oh My

No way, Gar.

It'll be fun.

You had fun. Admit it.
I guess it was kind of fun.
I know you loved it.
Tomorrow you'll be begging me to buy you a cowboy hat.
Why did I say *tomorrow?* Play it cool.
Doubtful.
Is she talking about the hat or seeing me tomorrow?

It's now or never.
I don't have any plans tomorrow. You?
Nope.
GUITAR
MOTEL
Want to check out some more places? We could meet here at eleven.
Twelve.
And no cowboy hats.

CHAPTER 5: ATHENA, GODDESS OF NASHVILLE
4:00 P.M. THE NEXT DAY
We're almost there.
I don't like surprises.
No peeking.
I'm not.
You are.
Open them.
NASHVILLE
1779

The Parthenon in Nashville? That's so random...but also pretty cool.
It was built in 1897 for the Centennial Exposition.

Have you ever been to Greece?
I went to Sierra Leone as a kid, but I don't really remember it.
Other than that, Nashville is the only place I've been outside of Georgia. You?
I've seen a few Southern cities, like New Orleans.
Bourbo
Africa sounds amazing. How did you end up there?
My parents are viral research scientists. They work in vaccine development. How about yours?
My mom died a few months ago.
For You
Memories
See All
I'm sorry about your mom.
Thanks.

Whoa.
Athena. Goddess of wisdom, war, and handicrafts.
Athena
GODDESS OF WISDOM, WARFARE & HANDICRAFTS
Kong! No climbing on Athena.

It would be cool if the Greek gods and goddesses were real. If you had a problem, you could bring them a gift—like a pizza—and they'd help.
Not all of them. Some gods, like Hades, were violent and dangerous.
You're right. I'd rather *be* one of the gods. Then I could solve my own problems.

Only if you could control your powers.
She's right. My powers—or whatever they are—would be a lot cooler if I knew how to control them.
NASHVILLE
1779

Does your boyfriend mind that we're hanging out?
The person I'm meeting isn't my boyfriend. But if I *was* dating someone, he'd be the kind of guy who wouldn't care.
If there's a god of luck, I owe him one.
NASHVILLE
Then why'd you say you had a boyfriend?
NASHVILLE 1779
I didn't. You assumed and I chose not to correct you.

That's harsh. Am I that bad?
No. It just seemed easier.
My last relationship ended badly.
What happened?
He was hiding things from me.
NASHVILLE

Where are you, Raven?
Tonight will be special.
We have excellent seats in the theater.
This place is just like N.O.L.A.— too many ghosts.

LOS ANGELES

H.I.V.E needs them alive and unharmed.
HOLLYWOO
Scare the hell outta them to see if they use their powers, but don't hurt 'em. Got it.
I've got a redhead to follow.
81°

How would you rate sightseeing day two, on a scale of one to ten?
NASHVILLE
A solid eight-point-five.
Stay where you are and don't scream.

GASP

CHAPTER 6:
FIGHT RISK
NASHVILL

NASHVILLE
1779
No...not now. I can't change in front of her.
Gar? Are you okay?
I've gotta make it stop.

What's wrong?
I'm fine. I just need a minute.
NASHVIL
1779
Where did all this muscle come from?
His shoulder didn't feel like that when we danced together.

My head is pounding.
Maybe you bumped it. Let me see.
No! I mean... I'm fine. You should get out of here in case that guy comes back.
I'm not leaving you alone.
NASHVILLE
1779

He's hiding something.
What are you thinking, Gar?
I can't hear your thoughts, but your emotions are coming in loud and clear. You're scared.
What are you so afraid of?

Finally.
Gar, you're burning up. We need to get you to a doctor.

No doctors. Please.
I have a...condition. I just need rest.
Are you sure?
Yeah.
I'm getting us a cab. We'll be back at your hotel soon.

TAXI
Your friend better not throw up in my cab.
He's not drunk.
Whatever you say.
NASHVILLE
You're going to be okay.

Ole Opry
MOTEL
TAXI
We're almost there.
Your shirt is soaked.
A high fever is normal.

I'll get a cold towel.
I should've taken him to the hospital. I don't even know what's wrong with him.
TSSHH
What kind of condition do you have, Gar?
A chemical imbalance.

Feel better...
Feel like I'm dying.
You're going to be okay.
5 A.M.
At least he cooled off a little.
I'd better stay awake. My soul-self will watch over me, but I'm not sure that applies to Gar.

3 P.M. THE NEXT DAY
She stayed all night and took care of me.
I...I didn't mean to fall asleep. Are you okay?
Mmm-hmm.

What are you waiting for? You probably won't get another chance...

What am I doing?
Tommy was adorable and sweet, too, and he was spying on me the whole time we were together.
Want to tell me what happened last night?
I can't tell her the truth. She'll think I'm a freak.
When we lived in Sierra Leone, I contracted a rare disease called sakutia.
There was no cure, so my parents gave me an experimental serum to save my life.
Guess you could say it had side effects.
There's something you're not telling me.
Wanna tell me about the nightmare you had?
Keep your secret.

AAHHT
AAHH
AAHHT
It's after three. We slept all day. I have to meet my...friend at five.
I'm meeting mine at four forty-five. Gimme a minute to jump in the shower and I'll walk with you.
Don't give her a chance to say no.
What am I doing, Kong?

THIRTY MINUTES LATER
I'm meeting my... friend near the cemetery. How about you?
Not far from the Grand Ole Opry. It woulda been cool if we were going to the same place.
Where are you, Raven?
Finally!
Of course she's gone. That light took *forever* to turn.

Will you give me your number? We can text or something.
Sure.
I'm really glad we met.
ROBIN ST
STOP
Me too.

Must be Slade.
Wait!
EEEK

Get off me!
Shut up.
What is—?
That'll keep you quiet.
I don't feel so good.

CHAPTER 7: SPECIAL OPS
CALL ME WHEN YOU GET SICK OF LIVING IN YOUR FATHER'S SHADOW AND YOU WANT TO DO SOME GOOD.
(555) 321 2040
Slade
A girl my age waiting on the same deserted street corner where I'm supposed to meet Slade in thirty minutes... coincidence?
Doubt it.
ROBIN ST
STOP
Let's see if anyone shows up to meet you, goth girl.

ROBIN ST
Maybe Gar will call.
Stop thinking about him. He wouldn't have felt the same way about me if he'd known the truth about what I am.
05:05
Focus on meeting Slade and getting answers.
But I don't have a good feeling about this.
That's what Trigon would want you to think.
What if he's growing stronger?
Getting close to Gar could've weakened my defenses against Trigon.
I can't let him get in my head again.

PARKING
Maybe they went this way.
Raven!

ROBIN ST
STOP
Who's in the van?
Don't touch me!
Stop!

What the hell is that?
STOP
SCRREEEECH

Only one way to find out.

Oh my god! Gar? Can you hear me?
What did you do to him?
Shut up or you'll find out firsthand.
It'd be my pleasure.

I have to concentrate and pay attention to what my soul-self sees.
Maybe I can figure out where they're taking us.

The van is getting too far ahead of me.
But I can still follow Raven's soul-self.
She's gone.

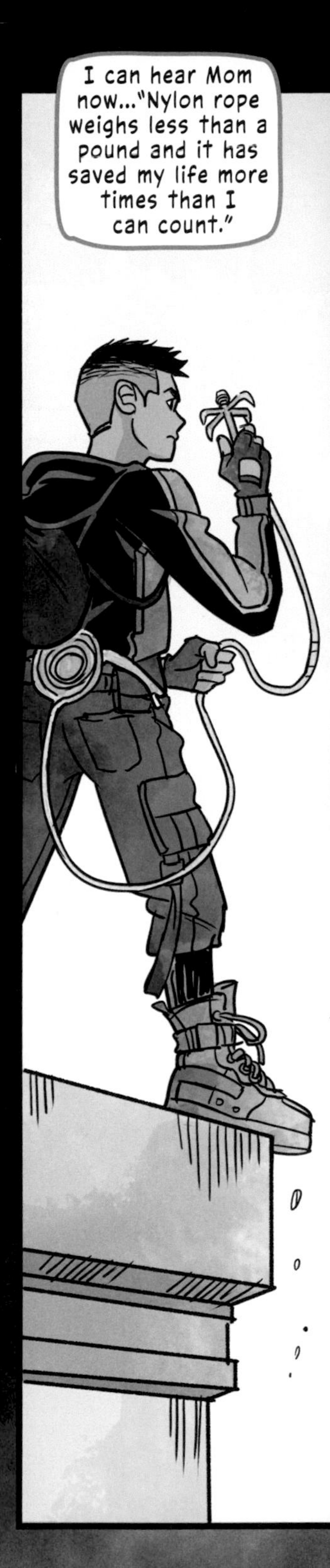
I can hear Mom now..."Nylon rope weighs less than a pound and it has saved my life more times than I can count."

It's annoying to have a black-ops-trained, hyper-vigilant mom who's always right.

Time to do some recon and figure out who Mystery Girl is and what she knows.

Gar?
Wake up.

Raven? I must be dreaming... going back to sleep.
You're not dreaming.
Raven... you're really here.
Who are those guys? Traffickers?
I don't want to hang around and find out.
Turn your hand toward mine.
I can't loosen the zip tie.

Come on...channel a gorilla or something and break them.
It won't open.
Maybe your friend will call the cops when you don't show up to meet him.
Slade? I doubt it. We aren't really friends. I've never even met him.
Long story.
The guy I was supposed to meet is named Slade, too. That can't be a coincidence.

I bet he set us up.
Why?
No idea. But I plan to find out.
Stop messing around and hurry. We've gotta unload them.
They're coming. Pretend you're asleep.
We're gonna be okay, Raven. I promise.

CHAPTER 8: STRATEGIC MANEUVERS
How am I going to find Raven now?
When I get my hands on that boy, he's in a world of trouble.
I'm looking for someone, too. Did you see a gray van?
It took a left at the end of the block.
Who are you talking to, Mystery Girl? Unless...

What's she doing, Mom?
Asking the spirits for guidance.
She must be talking to spirits like the old woman on the mountain.
I wonder what it's like to have a power like that...or *any* power.
I'll never know.

Raven could still be in there.
STOP
Please don't let me get caught.
Easy...
...does it.

Where are you, Raven?
Who's Raven?
Who the hell are you?

I was about to ask you the same question.
I'm happy to call the cops if you'd rather tell them.
911
If you were gonna call them, you woulda done it when the guys in the van grabbed your friend.
Who were they?
No clue. But I think the person your friend Raven was waiting for is the same guy I was supposed to meet.

My foster *sister.*
Whatever. Take a look.
Slade. That's who Raven was meeting.
Why should I trust you? How do I know you aren't in on it?
I've been accused of lots of things, but kidnapping isn't one of them.
We both need to find your foster sister. I'm assuming she has powers, too.
Excuse me?
I saw the bird shadow above the van and you talking to your ghost friends. Relax. You two aren't the only ones with powers.

I'll play along. What kind of power do you have?
Enhanced speed and reflexes and superior hand-to-hand combat skills.
What's this?
An infrared thermal scanner that picks up heat signatures.
It looks like a thermometer.
To the untrained eye, maybe.

What does Slade mean by "when you get sick of living in your father's shadow"?
My dad is a rich tech genius who thinks he's a hero. He's also a jerk. I grew up with my mom.
I've got something.
BEEEP
Let's keep looking.

CHAPTER 9: MONKEY BUSINESS
EEK EEK
Run, Kong!

Who are you guys?
No talking.
Home sweet home.
Ow!
What the—?

Crap!
I wonder what they injected us with.
A sedative, most likely.
So I can't use my powers? I'm being paranoid. How would they know about my powers?
They just want to keep us calm.
The question is ***why?***
HYPE

SLADE
Where are you?
BUZZ
It's from Slade. He's asking where I am.
DAMIAN
save it. i saw what happened to the girl.
SLADE
I'm looking for her, too.
Do you believe him?
Not even a little.

I'm gonna take a look around.
Could he be more annoying?
SNAPPP
EEEK
A monkey in a shirt?
Hold on...I recognize that T-shirt.

Hey, little guy. You know Raven, don't you?
EEEK
MEAT IS
I don't see anything except trees.
I found something.
A monkey?
Is he wearing clothes?

He belongs to a guy Raven has been hanging out with.
Think he was involved in your foster sister's kidnapping?
GUM
At this point, anything is possible.
Why wouldn't the monkey be with him?
Good question.
Do you know where to find Raven and your owner?

I think he wants us to follow him.
EEK EEK
I need a minute.
Guessing you're not on the track team.

Funny.
I might need more than a minute.
I'm not training for a future in special forces.
ZOOOMM

Ahhh!
What is *wrong* with you?
Timber rattler. One bite is venomous enough to kill a person.
Now what were you saying about my training?
If you're waiting for me to thank you, don't hold your breath.

We've gotta figure out who those people are.
CHAPTER 10: COMMON DENOMINATOR
Slade is the common denominator.
Why were you meeting him?
He used to work with my parents at H.I.V.E. He said he could help with my condition.
How about you?
He claimed to have information about my father, but that was probably a lie.
We're in serious trouble, Gar.

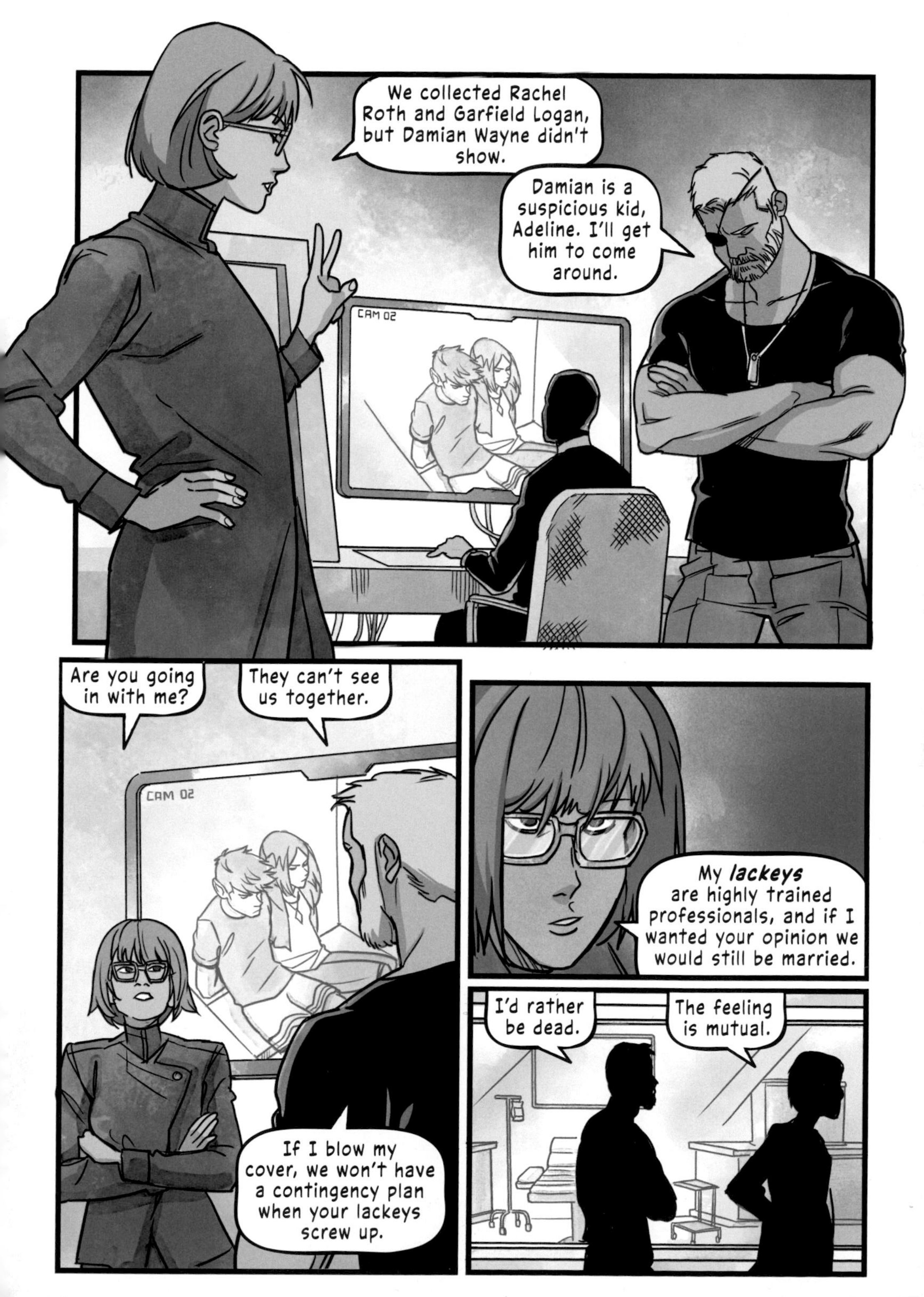
We collected Rachel Roth and Garfield Logan, but Damian Wayne didn't show.
Damian is a suspicious kid, Adeline. I'll get him to come around.
CAM 02
Are you going in with me?
They can't see us together.
CAM 02
If I blow my cover, we won't have a contingency plan when your lackeys screw up.
My *lackeys* are highly trained professionals, and if I wanted your opinion we would still be married.
I'd rather be dead.
The feeling is mutual.

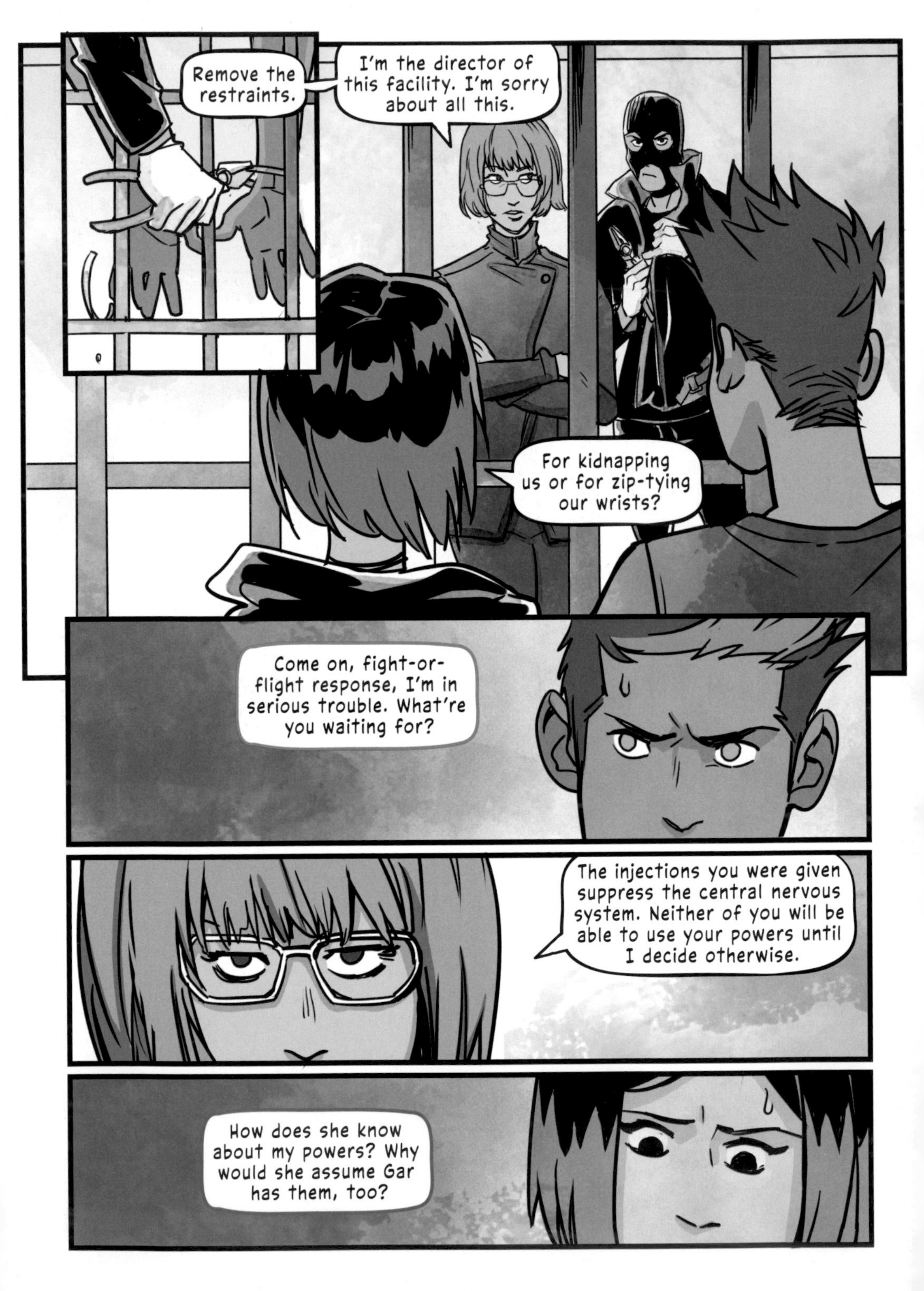
Remove the restraints.
I'm the director of this facility. I'm sorry about all this.
For kidnapping us or for zip-tying our wrists?
Come on, fight-or-flight response, I'm in serious trouble. What're you waiting for?
The injections you were given suppress the central nervous system. Neither of you will be able to use your powers until I decide otherwise.
How does she know about my powers? Why would she assume Gar has them, too?

Why does she think Raven has powers, and how'd this lady find out about mine?
I don't know what you're talking about, lady. What do you want from us?
You don't know about each other's powers, do you? Interesting.
As for what I want, the world is a cruel place for those of us who lack your gifts. With your help, I can change that.
Don't trust her, Raven. She wants to imprison us.
You're already imprisoned, Trigon. And there's no *us.*
I don't know how you're communicating with me, but it ends now.
We're not who you think we are, and even if we were, we wouldn't help you.
What she said.
I'll give you some time to think about it.

What is this thing?
A batarang. I stole it from my dad before I bailed.
Does he know where you are?
He has never even sent me a birthday card.
He wouldn't care.
EEEK

Did you see anything?
Some sort of facility...medical or military, maybe. It's hard to tell.
I need to take a closer look.
You mean **we** do.

A FEW MINUTES LATER
Stay here.
Like I'm going to listen to him.
Who are these people?

I've got a bad feeling about this.
The front entrance is covered by two armed guards. And don't say you told me to stay here. I'm not a dog.
The place is crawling with security. We'd need an army to go in there.
I might know where to find one.

CHAPTER 11: GHOST WHISPERER
TWO HOURS LATER
What are we doing back here?
Here goes...
Remember when you said you thought I had powers?
I can communicate with the dead and harness their power.
Are you saying you can raise a ghost army?
Not exactly.

I can communicate with the dead and channel their power, but my mom does the raising part.
We're kind of a team.
Concentrate. You got this.
Why are you touching me? Ever heard of consent?
Sorry. Trying to help with motivation.
If you touch me again without permission, I'll help your arm into a cast.
Just a heads-up...if this works you'll be able to see the ghosts. It happens when you raise them.

What does Mom always say?
I call you—mothers, daughters, sisters, and grandmothers, warrior women in this cemetery—from your restful sleep.
Help me save Raven.
RUMMBBBLE
I call you—mothers, daughters, sisters, and grandmothers, warrior women in this cemetery...
Help me save Raven.
CRRAAACH

You're doing it!
RIIPPP
The shaking and cracking stopped.
It's over.
You almost had it. Try again.
It didn't work. End of story.

Where are we going?
Wait! Where are you taking her?
You okay?
Yeah.
SPSSHHH
That can't be good.

Cover your mouth!
MUSIC ON WORLD OFF
Why is my heart beating so fast? And my pulse is racing.
Gar!
MUSIC ON WORLD OFF
What's happening to him?

Gar?
This is what was happening to him the night he got sick.

PSSHH
Gar? Are you okay?
No more.
Not sure how much more of this I can take.

Stop! You're hurting him!
MUSIC ON WORLD OFF
I can help you, daughter.
You're imagining his voice. Ignore it.

FOUR HOURS LATER
SPSSHHHH
Please...make it stop.
CLICKK

PLEASE ADOPT
I'm scared.
Help me.
It's so cold.
I want my mom.
PLEASE ADOPT
Fear.
Hunger.

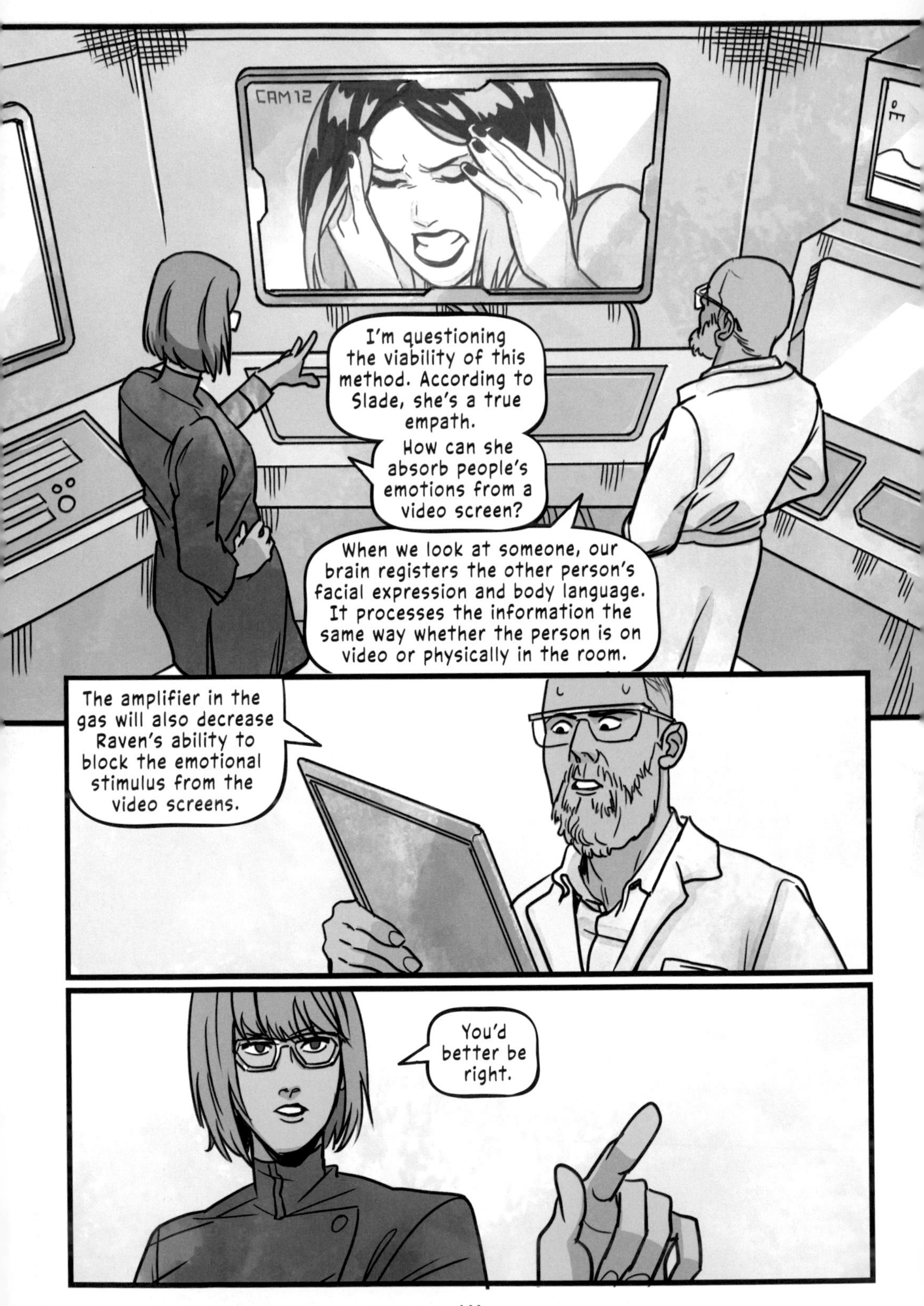
CAM 12
I'm questioning the viability of this method. According to Slade, she's a true empath.
How can she absorb people's emotions from a video screen?
When we look at someone, our brain registers the other person's facial expression and body language. It processes the information the same way whether the person is on video or physically in the room.
The amplifier in the gas will also decrease Raven's ability to block the emotional stimulus from the video screens.
You'd better be right.

Too many voices...
How am I absorbing their emotions?
MUSIC ON WORLD OFF
Raven? What's happening?
Make it stop.

What the hell?

I'm here, Raven. Look at me.
I'll do whatever you want, just leave her alone.
Gar...don't.
I knew you'd come around.

CHAPTER 12: UNEXPECTED GUESTS
Don't beat yourself up. The bodies were buried under six feet of dirt.
My mom could've pulled that off in her sleep.
I know what it's like to have parents who are badasses.
My mom would've had us inside the facility by now. She could take out four or five guards on her own. Same with my father.
Thanks.
I could call Mom, but what if Raven is running out of time?
We can't overpower the kidnappers, so we'll have to outsmart them.

DAWN
Unless you know how to scale walls, the loading dock is the easiest way in.
When the guard circles around the truck, you're gonna follow me.
Got it.

Work fast.
You first.

At least she didn't argue with me for once.
I think Kong knows where he's going.

I *hope* this monkey knows where he's going.
C'mon, Max. I'll catch you.
I don't need help.
Don't be stubborn.

THUMMPP
Oh man...she's beautiful.
You okay?
Yeah. Sorry.
Were his eyes always this green? And why does it feel so nice to have his hands on my hips?
Do not get butterflies over him.

Damian...
Relax. We're leaving.
CLICK
Don't move.
On your knees.
Hands behind your backs.

Don't beat yourself up. The bodies were buried under six feet of dirt.
But those bodies aren't.
I call you to join me. I need your help.
Max...

Stay back!

Don't hurt me.
Then keep your mouth shut.

CHAPTER 13: RECKONING
It's over. I'm okay.
They are not finished with you.
You're okay.
Please be okay.
Did I ever mention how much I love wolves and cheetahs?

I should probably tell you that I have a thing for giant shadows shaped like ravens.
I wish you'd told me about your... condition.
It doesn't freak you out?
It's part of you, and I like all of you.

With all due respect, Ms. Kane, I think they've had enough.
That's for me to decide.
They won't be of any use to you if they're dead.
I have to break them or reconditioning will be too difficult—especially Raven.

There's something I should tell you about my powers.
How do I tell him I'm a monster?
SPSSH
No more... please.
Stop it!

Gar! You're killing him!
I don't have enough strength left.
MUSIC ON WORLD OFF
WROOAAARR

There's only one way I can save him. I have to open up to Gar and let myself feel everything.
If I release you, Trigon, you have to help me save my friend.
It will be done. Our fates are bound. Free me and you will free yourself.
I decide my fate, and right now I'm using it to save Gar.

MUSIC ON
ORLD OFF

BOOOOMMMm
What is that thing?
Who cares! Shoot it!

Your pathetic mortal toys cannot harm me.
Dear god. What are we looking at?
Future defense technology, if we can get our hands on it.

MUSIC ON
WORLD OF
SMASHHH

Am I seeing what I think I'm seeing? 'Cuz that looks like a monster.
Meet Raven's dad. Technically, he's a demon.
Positions!
Particle dispersers on!

I've gotta help her. What good is this power if I can't use it to help the girl I'm crazy about?

This is *my* body, and for once, it's gonna listen to *me.*
RWRAWR

No!

Go, Max!

What are you doing here?
Saving you.
Who's he?
Her new boyfriend.
He is *not* my boyfriend.
Yet.

CHAPTER 14:
DIRTY LAUNDRY
THREE HALLWAYS LATER
LAUNDRY
In there!
Go! Go! Go!

Look for a car that's unlocked.
Found one! Come on!

How'd you learn to hot-wire a car?
My mom.
TSSTT

I still don't understand how you knew where to find me, Max. And how did you meet this guy?
It's a long story. I followed you from N.O.L.A. because I was worried.
I saw the men grab you, but I was too far away to do anything about it.
Ditto. I was on the roof of the building doing recon. I was supposed to meet Slade an hour later.
Damian Wayne, by the way.
Recon? Okay...
I'm Gar. Thanks for the help back there.

Do you know what those people were planning to do with you two?
They were interested in our powers. My guess is they're involved in human trafficking.
MUSIC ON
Or they're doing experiments for the military or a pharmaceutical company.
I wonder where that dirtbag Slade is right now.

ROSE BOWL FLEA MARKET
LOS ANGELES, CA
Rose Bowl
Adeline?
I knew your second-rate mercenaries would screw up.
But I have a contingency plan.

We should find somewhere to lay low in case they're looking for us.
Campground
We all need some rest, too. I'm wrecked.
Turn there.
I could sleep for a week.

What if they're looking for us, Gar?
They won't find us out here, but I won't let anyone hurt you.
Even though you were the one who rescued me.
We rescued each other.
You were pretty great in the morgue.
You did okay, too.

HOURS LATER
We can crash out here tonight, but tomorrow we'll need to find somewhere safe to go.
My parents would help, but I'm not really talking to them.
And I'm not sure I'm ready to start.
I'd never ask my dad for help, and my mom is out of the country.
Not that she'd trust them enough to help.
My mom will help us, and she knows about my powers, and Raven's.

She said *us* like she's including me.
Chill, Damian. A girl like Max isn't interested in you.
I'll call my mom in the morning. I don't have the energy to explain what happened and why I didn't call her sooner.
She'll understand.

I'll keep watch.
Go to sleep. We're in the woods and Gar has tiger hearing.
More like bat or moth hearing. They're way better.

I can't sleep.
Me neither.
MUSIC ON WORLD OFF
She'll never believe me when I tell her they were spooning.
Proof.

What are we gonna do about those people and the...um...
The demon. You can say it.
His name is Trigon. He's my father.
MUSIC ON WORLD OFF
I don't care, if that's what you think. You saw me turn into... well...you know.
I think it's cool. I just wish you had told me, but I understand why you didn't.
It started a few months ago. I can't really control it.

At least it's not creepy like my power...or whatever you want to call it.
MUSIC ON ...LD OFF
I call it amazing...like you.
My father is a *demon,* Gar. And I set him free.
Who knows where he is or what he's doing.
MUSIC ON
You saved my life.
We'll figure out the rest. We're in this together.
I really wanna kiss you right now.
I don't want you to get hurt.

Then don't hurt me.
Don't kiss me unless you're okay with me the way I am—not just the cool parts of me, but the messy, mixed-up, imperfect parts, too.
I like it all, Raven. And I like who I am when I'm with you.
I'm gonna count to three before I kiss you. So if you're not sure how you feel about me, this is your out.
One. Two.
Three.

kami garcia

is the #1 *New York Times*, *USA Today*, and international bestselling co-author of the Beautiful Creatures and Dangerous Creatures novels. *Beautiful Creatures* has been published in 50 countries and translated into 39 languages. Kami's solo series, The Legion, includes *Unbreakable*, an instant *New York Times* bestseller, and its sequel, *Unmarked*, both of which were nominated for Bram Stoker Awards. Her other works include *The X-Files Origins: Agent of Chaos* and the YA contemporary novels *The Lovely Reckless* and *Broken Beautiful Hearts*. Kami was a teacher for 17 years before co-authoring her first novel on a dare from seven of her students. She is a cofounder of YALLFest, the biggest teen book festival in the country. She lives in Maryland with her family.

gabriel picolo

is a Brazilian comics artist and illustrator based in São Paolo. His work has become known for its strong storytelling and atmospheric colors. Picolo has developed projects for clients such as Blizzard, BOOM! Studios, HarperCollins, and DeviantArt. His first graphic novel, *Teen Titans: Raven*, was a *New York Times* bestseller.

Constantine is not your average bad boy...

John Constantine is, and has always been, a magician of the highest caliber—
who doesn't need additional training from any high-brow magician, thank you very much.
Sensing an opportunity for independence, Constantine falsely accepts an apprenticeship
in the United States to become the lead singer of his best friend's punk band, Mucus Membrane.
When the band begins to dabble in magic, a complicated spell gets out of hand...
and the disastrous consequences might be more than Constantine can handle.

Keep reading for a sneak peek of ***Constantine: Distorted Illusions***,
by **Kami Garcia** and **Isaac Goodhart**!

Art not final.

London
I rang Lady Marguerite Delphine in the States today about some society business. Seems she's accepting another apprentice.
He told her you're taking a year off before university.
A year off that doesn't include studying magic with a highbrow magician from Roderick's society—the equivalent of a coven for magicians.
I'm not interested in being an apprentice.

I just thought you might—
You thought wrong.
John...
I hate disappointing my mum, even though she's probably used to it by now.
Sorry, Mum.
John, wait.

Dulles International Airport, Virginia
Three Days Later
Constantine! Over here!

I forgot how good-looking you are.
I bet you're regretting the friends-without-benefits pact we made.
Actually, I was thinking about all the guys who'll want to steal me when they think you're my boyfriend.
Hopefully, one of them will have a car.
TAXI
No time to look for one. I've had back-to-back gigs since graduation.

That's Georgetown in Washington, D.C. My apartment isn't far.
My roommate is the band's bassist. He's a pain in the ass, but he's into magic. My aunt moved to L.A., so I can't afford to be picky.
Veronica's parents aren't around. They make my dad look like father of the year.

Home not-so-sweet home.

Helloooo! *We're back!*
What up? Christian Slaughter. Everyone calls me Slaughter.
I've met guys like him before—guitarists who think they're Sid Vicious.
John.
Everyone calls him Con-stan-teen 'cuz it rhymes with *mean.*
Not really.
Heard you're a magician. Maybe you can teach me some tricks.
Not the kind of magic I do.

It's a joke, man. I've got magicians in my family. I'm into occult stuff.
Right.
He's worse than I thought.
I'm filling in for a hardcore band at Riot. They're down a bassist and they need a pro.
Later, mate.

Tomorrow do you wanna rehearse or check out D.C.?
I'm supposed to meet Lady Marguerite, but I can reschedule. It's not like I'm gonna train with her.
Meet her before you decide. I'd kill to have a teacher.
Thought you needed a lead singer? Trying to get rid of me already?
I meant at the end of the summer. Don't be a baby. But I don't want you to blow an opportunity.

What's wrong?
I'm bloody late.
Thought you didn't care about meeting the magician?
BLACK COFFEE
I don't, but I promised my mum I'd meet her.
Has anyone ever told you that you're confusing?
Not today.
CONSTANTINE: DISTORTED ILLUSIONS COMING FALL 2022
BLACK